MW01596394

The

In-Between

Moments

Written By: Authentic

Intelligence

Aka Daniel A. Hall

Introduction

In brainstorming what this piece of work would be, I often sat with the relationship I shared with poetry. The ups and downs, the ins and outs, as well as the beauty and mundane aspects of this passion. I thought back to my previous projects and the poems I concocted, with wide-eyed wonder, and thought how different poetry felt. It was a vibrant landscape of infinite possibilities and choices, and I was an energized child ready to bask in the spoils it presented me. However, as I matured in poetry, that once abundant soil seemed to hide its treasures from me. The work became harder. Each poem felt like I was mining for gold nuggets and picking away at ideas I combed through a million times before.

So, I took a break from poetry, as an art form. I delved into music and photography to broaden my artistic lens. I also made a proactive decision to experience life because I felt as though the first two projects had consumed me. I wanted to have experiences and not feel obligated to draw inspiration from them.

It was weird, not going to lie. It felt like I was just "in the mix". A passive viewer watching the friends, family, and all other people around him make moves in their artistic expressions. Don't get me wrong, I was extremely thrilled for them, and cheered them on every chance I could. I was just not able to tap into whatever (seemingly) endless source they had. I was the space in between the stanzas, waiting for my next line break; and an idea was born.

A lot of people would ask me,

"When's the next book coming out?"

"What's it going to be about?"

"Do you have any ideas of what you'll do with this next one?"

And, if I'm quite honest, I never had a concrete answer. In the past three years, the response had essentially boiled down to *"Not sure yet, but it's cookin'! Be on the lookout!"* I wanted this trifecta of a book to mean as much to me as its priors did (and still do), so I was intentional on how I would go about it.

So, my dear reader, this is what I've come to understand from my break from poetry, my venturing into different creative outlets, and from choosing to live proactively: there will always be an in-between moment. There will inevitably be days where it will feel like you are in a midst, instances in which you'll be in the middle of your mountaintop and your valley. In spite of this, I implore to see it through a different lens. The pit stops in any journey will make the destination seem farther than it is. I've come to learn that it's all about perspective. Poems without line breaks would just be lengthy ramblings. Essays without indents are just blobs of vocabulary. So take your time, give yourself grace, and don't be afraid to live a little. The good things take patience and perseverance.

I hope these musings resonate with you the way they've resonated with me. Most importantly, I pray that this book is to you what it's been to me; a means to dig deeper into yourself, and ask yourself the questions you may have waited too long to ask.

Until next time, always remember; Stay Beautiful, Stay Safe, & Stay Authentic!

- To my family, friends, and all others that have seen gift mature, grow, and thrive;

I love you & thank you for your continued support!

Three's Company

I've been told this is supposed to be my trifecta;
My tried and true.
A ménage à trois of ideas from the same lover of poetry.
That this is, supposedly, supposed to be my chance to see
what I could make of a three-peat
A golden opportunity, stated clearly by my peers and
followers.
But what if hollow words were all that came out?
What if I hallowed verses, only for them to be gilded and
perverse
Worshipped like a truth I can no longer relate to?

This is the third iteration of my matrix,
A lost soul trying to not only be found, but be heard
All while facing its own tune.
Whether the melody becomes a tragedy, romance, or
something in between
I want you to know I meant well.

I just hope the notes of these songs give another being solace.
I hope my lyrics,
Written with honest intentions,
Lead to the aforementioned blessings
Not yet seen, but ever so often heard, somewhere in these words...

Lyricism

If you're hearing this
It's probably because someone forced to you
Or coerced you to
If you're hearing this
It's mostly likely to see if I have the mastery to make
sentence structures submissive
Or even to see if I carry the missive that I claim to
If you're listening to this
I do not really blame you for your lack of support
Just because there are times where I seem out of sorts
If you're here
Hearing this right now
Wow, I didn't think you'd make it this far onto the track
I know most would consider the limber technique of poetry
pointless
That it proves nothing
A dead art form for your grandparents or something
You might think it's wanting to wager words to woo
women

That it probably wouldn't even make me enough to cop the
linen on my back
Perhaps
You just don't get it

So instead,
You jettison your confusion into the conclusion that poetry
is wack
That attacking prose ain't as tough
As packin' gats and serving O's
And I don't know, maybe that's valid
Maybe poetic stanzas prove to be too pallid for your mind
Not enough color added to bind or bring light to your
imagination
It could very well be, that it just isn't some's forte
This could be in poor taste, hoping to be the paste to hold
lyricism together

A Writer's Wondering

I wonder,
What am I without my words ?

Without pen to paper
Or palm to psalm?

Do I savor life the same way ?

Are sunrises still as beautiful when I don't have the
vocabulary to describe it?

What happens when the scribe no longer needs to be
prescribed diatribe to combat his inner thoughts?

How does the way I perceive alter what cascades on a
page like dripping water?

Will the daughter cells of past iterations still process
things through my own senses?

Or will these descendants of my old verses not need prose to grow?

I'd like to think that I know but, really, does anyone?

Or are we stuck asking questions we'll only get answers to, long after they're asked?

New World

I feel like a hypocrite

Like all the words I've ever written have someone else's heart smitten.

As if the inked curves I once held near and dear to my core have left me for a better poet...

Lord knows I know it doesn't make much sense

But ever since this world changed, it seems as though I have been with it.

I know that should be good

And I wish I could be more specific, but the words don't find me the way they used to;

Spruced and packaged on my doorstep, more or less

I don't impress myself the way I once did

The poems don't form like I want them to

I'm constantly circling around the future

And the past

Because the present doesn't last long enough for me.

Days blur, suggesting that my temporal eyesight ain't what it used to be.

Maybe there's no use in chasing yesterday

Or tomorrow

Reliving sorrows you can't change

Nowadays, words are either miraculously marinating in myriads

Or halted like tunes stopped by 39.532 second ads

Times an infinite amount of possibilities to fit on this page

In that note

In that mental cage, blotched out

A figure wandering through haze

A dazed and lost soul

Hoping for something to make him whole

My heart,

Swollen for this concept,

Would cry out

But the drought of tears leaves me feeling like

I can no longer feel

What's real?

Because if these words aren't

I don't know that this new world could ever be

Late Night Laments

Past passions perceptively pass over this persona

Like an iota inside an immeasurable idea

An abstract anomaly, absent anywhere that attracts
attention

Maybe my mind is mistaken,

And everything emanating from this ethereal entity that
is my existence is exactly what ought to be expected;

A reflection of the riveting and robust nature that runs
through me

But the blistering barrage of battles beneath my bold
exterior breaks bits of my being

And chisels chunks of my character until catharsis comes & changes the concentration in which I conceptualize care

Causing me to contemplate the course I've committed to

Well, then, what words would I write?

Which works of mine will writhe my worries from me?

When the wordsmith wakes from the wearisome process,

Where will the watchers and witnesses wait with wonder-filled eyes?

Roaming Thoughts

Internally isolating the impressions I'd idly ignore

Isn't instilling the idealistic intrigue it once did.

Instead, it imposes an idolized impasse inside

Indicating the ions of my irises are impeded by my
impotent imagination...

I wish the words flowed more freely.

Perhaps then, I'd probably pass fewer pessimistic pardons

Or the plethora of personal pleas to put pen to paper
wouldn't plague me persistently...

I miss the times when my lyrics came alive.

Strutting successfully across sanctuaries of scrap paper

Seeking solace in the secret slivers of spare sidelines on scattered sheets of sacred nights

Scarcity is something I never saw my sentences succumbing to.

What if I'm losing it...?

What would I do when the weight of words wanders from me?

Would I worry, wondering who it went to?

Or would I will myself to wait, woefully wincing at the wistful way in which my soul waned?

Flow

If no more words find themselves across this page
All I hope is that this phase of completion complements
everything before it.
I hope I'll be able to absorb it as poetic musings,
separated from me
All I can ask is that this mask be fitted to someone else's
dome
That these words will find another home with someone
who appreciates them more than I ever could

If this poet has completely left the pen on the pad,
I'm unironically glad of the way it comes to a close.
Hopefully, these prose will be a map for souls trying to
make sense of things.
I really want this to bring peace, not only to me but to
every iteration of my genes that deems these pages worthy
of their attention.

I wish for these lyrics to be a recollection when needed
Words to be heeded

All I can aspire to do is inspire the few that want to be,
and offer my two cents to the riches of mankind:

What really matters?
Are we our emotions?
What's it like to give meaning to patterns?

I don't know for sure what I hope to gain from these
pages of poetry
All I know is that it'd be cool to have it flow through
audiences
As it flowed through me

Sensitivity

There are days when being a sensitive soul takes a toll on
me.
I feel as though I can't hold conversations
And I take everything too personally
Even though I know that I shouldn't

I know it's been said to be a gift
That it means we're well-versed in sympathy
But sometimes, it feels like it just causes a rift in me.
I can't say what I want
Without the taunt of someone laughing
Or shrugging me off
Or hugging me, telling me I ought not take things to heart
But how can I not when I wear it on my sleeve?

They say it takes time to harness the power of sensitivity
And maybe I'm just not there yet
Because every piece of luggage I carry with me seems too
heavy for anyone else to bear.
Sharing seems overrated

Talks of what goes on in my head feel like a debated controversy
Or, better yet, a conspiracy
Where I deliriously consider others above myself
Speaking my mind seems more like a waste of breath
Than a weight off my chest

So, most days, it feels better to suffer in silence
Than to try to make the violence of sensitivity make sense.
These thoughts tack on too much dense and tense energy
for me to comfortably speak my truth

... My Truth...

Huh, funny
It feels more like lies about how my body believes it's being treated
Like I'm seated at the mercy of the world's court to decide if anything I feel holds merit
Like, I'll get a carrot for the views from my caged conscious

Perhaps it might be a curse

Forever trapped between every convo

Every verse

Every page

Lasting longer in every perverse part of my perception

The rage I feel from the insane and deranged parts of me

that want to scream to cry

But I lie and say, "Ohh, don't worry about it. I'm okay,
I'm fine."

But am I?

COLORS

... Some days, I'm just a metaphor
Floored by his flaws
A sentence structure stuck
Feeling like there's no clause
Stagnant in his why's
But never really focus on "because"
Maybe because wise is what I'm hoping I can touch
Some days I'm a paragraph of galaxies
On other days just a part of speech
A fallacy
Casually trying to make sense of myself
And find dollars hidden on shelves
I cannot seem to reach
Some days I wanna teach
Some days I want each and every word I've ever written
Committed to memory
Sometimes I wonder what my legacy is
Just because I've planted many seeds,
Unaware of the fruit they've produced
Other days, I think of living out my days as a recluse

With only my poems and the walls to keep me company...

Some days I feel abundantly blessed
Caressed by the hand of the Most High
Some days I cry, thinking I'm just a little too flawed
Some days I'm afraid that the colors will do me in
That green will stare me into monstrous envy
Beige will batter me beneath submission
Missing all the golden hues I was looking forward to
Red will cause a meltdown in me,
So ferocious it would make nuclear clouds look like cotton
candy
Surely, these surly colors would be to blame for my demise
But no
They get to play the game
win the prize
While I deal with all the rules and consequences
 I'd have to build up fences
And relentlessly fight
Push my way through the amalgamation of pigments
Figments and personifications of things that "aren't that
deep"

Black would be my only haven
Not because it would be
Saving me from colors
I'd just avoid them completely
And discreetly look for peace in the absence of actions
caused by shades and hues

Some days, I'm afraid the colors will take me
Make me into something that only holds a fraction of
myself
That on certain days
The grays will dominate
Leaving me an empty husk
Rolling through a bustling world until the sun goes down
For it's then,
When the world sleeps
That these blues
Will fuel the cogs in my insomnia
Spinning out of control
Bold and boisterous instruments
Refusing to let my soul rest

Some days,
I'm afraid that the colors will break me
That the rainbow will be too much
That these abstracts will hit like concrete falling from the
sky
And I won't be strong enough to lift them
Or quick enough to move out of its way
I fear I might fray or fold
But I look for gold or silver linings
Hoping my mining isn't in vain
But I wouldn't dare ask to be plain
Because colors are the window pane
That paints the view
The hues make you who you are
It's hard
But it is what it is

Some days, I'm afraid the colors will do me in
But not today

LIFTED PRAYER

Lord, prepare my poems to turn into psalms.
Let every whistle of my epistles
Be a balm to my palms,
As well as a calm word to all those in need.
Let these words be devoid of all pride and any greed
Let those who read every single thought that I write
Have a lamp to guide their way through part of their
nights
Until they find You

God, allow my scribbles to be in tune with Your scripture
Purchase my soul from this world to renew and make
richer
The gifts that you've instilled in this mixture
Of flesh and spirit
Not the prettiest picture
But at least I'm Yours
At least You know most of my intentions are pure
And in the times I fall short
It's always on You that I call

To be sure that I haven't strayed too far from Your grace
And extensive mercies

From temptation, anger, and greed
Give me a new sight with every drop of this ink
Don't allow me to think that I know better
With every poem, let it alter my view
So every time that I make a choice
It'll be a reflection of You

I don't know what else to do to talk to You
So I'm jotting my feelings down like David did
Hoping that You hear from me as much as I long to hear
from You

Annual Wish

All I can hope for
Is more sunny days
More funny ways to view the ordinary
To see the scary parts as a very convoluted path to
simplicity

All I can ask is that the intricacies that make me myself
Continue to live in gifts like the present
I want to stay present for every moment that'll make my
soul smile
And for every mile these shoes travel
To contain millions of gravel-sized pieces of wisdom

All I can inquire
Is that every schism inside me can retire
So I can collect the pension for the years I've spent
working on myself
I hope whatever I have left
Can be used to sow seeds
And everyone can reap the benefits of this wealth

All I can pray
Is for more days of learning and unlearning certain
behaviors
To do favors without asking for limelights
Or reciprocated labors
To get closer to my Savior

All I want
Is for everyone to have better decades
For y'all to wake up every morning and feel grateful for it
For the folks that need love
Or a hug
To find it
I'd love for us to discover what makes life worth it
To always recognize the perfect in all our "imperfections"

All I need is for us to be better reflections than the world
is us
If you can do that, then that'll be just fine

Ramblings (A Modern Proverb)

The funk will never die
It will just just multiply
And pack these packed-out spaces like a poltergeist
And alter minds
It will still hold a candlelight when other genres lose their
fights
And forever be the reason that a song will fly

But what do I know?
I'm just a Brooklynite 'tryna hit high notes
While everyone around me is obsessed with going viral
Being an idol
Knowing full well they don't deserve the title...
Excuse the flow
I guess the brain's just going idle

Maybe we're just hoping to make sense of what we're given
Busy surviving instead of living
Perhaps I'm smitten with all the music in my words
And praying that they serve

The bigger purpose in the world around us

But word

I'm just imbuing y'all with proverbs

'Til you get the message

The precious form of perceptive introspection

Or I could be opening up blessings by removing the
floodgates

And let you get the lesson

They say less is more that way

And every other iota is getting in the way

Of those nuggets of wisdom and knowledge that scholars
debate

The stuff that weighs heavy on the mental of
instrumental thoughts that'll offer parlays

And expose the biggest jack in the pot

Gambling everything they love

Just to spit nonsense in the spot

But luckily y'all have me

To weave around these false spitting banshees

'Fore they scream the rhetoric to a stop

These ramblings is all that I got

The only thing that makes this drop in the ocean

Feel like it's mixed with hyssop

To purify the waters

And leaving the game for sons and daughters

So they can always remember their pops

For re-experiencing the bops

And see the forest

Not only for the trees

But all the dreams

And possibilities that make their way from behind the

curtain and through the seams

Have you wondering,

"Are all these lyrics more than they seem?"

And maybe they are

I don't know

Perhaps the Father's shining His light

And I just glow as a byproduct

Not a high prophet

Just a lowly servant emptying his pocketed wordplay

For brighter days
You know what they say
Ohh you don't? Me neither
I just grab what I can from the Teacher
And pass it on to you
So we can be in tune like that lady that was always
singing the blues

Matter of fact, if you're reading this now this is a sign,

Everything good will come to you in time
All you have to do is spread your wings and fly
Let positivity take you, and you'll be just fine

An Anonymous Inquiry into the Writer's Mind

New work is often hard to create
Because it always goes through that vicious hate/love cycle
Or, even worse,
The verse becomes idle; stale.
Maybe the poet is expected to prevail
Perhaps they're meant to bounce back after a fail
Just as long as they pass off something as real...

New work often feels like a charlatan
A harlot banned for posing as something they are not.
It seldom feels like jotting down scattered particles on a
page even matters
It doesn't phase you.
Instead, it plays you like the most melancholy music ever
made...

CRUMPLED UP L*VE LETTERS

If you love me, then hug me
And if you hug me, it's bubbly
And if it's bubbly, it must be
And if it must be, then please darling never ever let go

While everybody's on Gina
I'm Tommy peaking at Pam
Running through my mind, got other thoughts on the lam
Fellas might say I'm tweaking
Know what? Maybe I am
The only person that's got me
Producing these prose by hand
In iambic pentameter
Written by an amateur
Like all of my stamina's
Captured, like mem'ries on camera

Just a subject
Looking for a predicate
Like heaven-sent spirits

All up in the firmament
Fervently fusing factions
Matching my words with my actions
Good man with a good heart,
Can you imagine?
Pursuing romantic passions
Regardless of all the lashings
That Cupid decides to fashion
To unbreak my heart like Braxton

Wait——
Let's try this one more time——

Don't mean to sound too cliche
But this a poem about love
Forgive me when I say, but
Ya boy done got the bug
(Yeah he done got the bug)

Ain't nothing new under sunshines
Except for the fun times you offer me
And it's all for free, except when I pay attention

To every inflection of things that make me smile
Like when you mention that you been
Peeping and sensing that a divine intervention
Is the reason these dimensions
Hold no tension for me anymore

This is a crumpled up l*ve letter
Discarded and put away
Until I can understand
What I really mean to say
Until I can love better
Until I unravel my flaws
Until we can heal together
Until we are ready to bloom
Despite storms that tried to weather
The bond between me and you
To a love that we'll always remember

If you love me, then hug me
And if you hug me, it's bubbly
And if it's bubbly, it must be
And if it must be, then please darling never ever let go

First word sounds like

Sunrises;
like the happy lives of childhoods under endless summer
skies
It feels like Friday afternoon
like new clothes on cleansed bodies
Like self-fulfilling hobbies that make your soul smile

First word feels like inner children blooming like buds from
rich soil
like that first real day of spring
First words bring life to otherwise haphazard situations
and circumstances
First words feel like second chances
almost as if grace and mercy curtsy at our arrival
Like our faith is placed in the abstract expressionism
that is verse

First word tastes like peace
like energy flowing from person to person
Like we're all just versions of the same idea

A world full of beacons
First word can sound like just speaking
But I'd like to think otherwise

The highest highs
The love in a parent's eyes
Winning the stuffed prize at carnivals after spending all
day on amusement park rides
Like the light inside knows who you are

Like the stars are envious of your shine...

Ring / Limit / Systems

... Maybe the ringing in our ears when it's silent is just
our deepest fears fighting for the forefront thought;
Acting out in the quiet places.

It could be our insecurities attempting to push us to our
limits,
Trying to shape and mold us to the point where the
amount of situations that plagues us are limited.
What if, after all that toiling, the only things left are the
uninhibited truths we tried so hard to run from.

It's interesting how we, being specks
Floating in systems of celestial bodies, will traverse
through love, laughter, and tragedies all to emphatically
stay with sanity.
It's as though we find sanctuary in the sanctity of where
we find ourselves
Wandering in sporadic rotations
Focusing on their ebbs and flows

I guess it goes to show that anything can grow from nothing
That the ringing in our ears is just to test the limits of the systems we are slaves to...

A Letter to your Inner Child

Hey you,

Do you remember when back in the day
All we had were endless possibilities
To be or do whatever we chose;until infinity?

We could do anything that we thought of
Minor or major, like be an astronaut, a chef, or the
mayor
Our dreams were our fuel
And all we had to do was ignite it
To sail seas or cruise the air like pirates and pilots
We could've been an actor, a lawyer, a teacher,
A scientist, a singer, a preacher
Or everything else under the sun

And we had all the dedication to get ALL of it done

But when did the dreams become too much to dare?

When was it that we started to care about the naysayers
who had nothing to share?
Who had nothing to add?
In what way was that fair?
To tell this child with infinite potential to just stick to
their square
Why did we budge and equivocate on our desires
Why'd we let the haters pour water on our fires
Instead we should've pushed back and told these defilers
That what doesn't kill us
Will only make us soar higher...

A Dreamer's Reminisce

... Reminiscing on the times where my rhymes seemed to come alive

Where passion pounced off the page

Back when the stages didn't feel like stages, they felt like platforms for conversations

I can't wait to get back to that feeling, but I know I gotta stay faithful and patient, because this dream is too true to not come to pass

So I raise a glass to the dreamers alike. This is for us never dowsing our light

For we know in the end, everything will be alright...

.Expectations.

Y'know, I feel like all we seem to have are expectations
Where we think and believe that our dreams have just
become vacant, barren version of themselves
Unwilling to remold and fit our current situations

It's as if we're facing all these thoughts of uncertainty
and doubt
Wondering if one day, we'll have all this figured out
And we could spout endless words of affirmation and
prayers
But it won't be until we apply ourselves that our goals will
prevail higher than we ever dared to hope for

In the end, it's all about subverting those expectations
So that in time, when we look back,
Everything was only recalibrating to that moment
We're in the bag all year, so own it
And for now, I hope that we can enjoy ourselves at our
present

Because we're only just beginning to realize our current blessings...

Midst

... Whenever I'm in the midst of anything
I always dread it
Midst? More like mist
Almost like a cloud or fog clogging up my vision
Like there's not enough track to get my train of thought
to the final destination... I don't know
I just feel like it's pointless; like sleeping with no dreams.
Doesn't that seem useless? Just about as bad as scarfing
down food just to be eating?
What's the point of it all?

Why is it that every middle feels like it's just that?
Never really knowing when you'll hit that turning point; an
occurrence to pull you one way or another
The midst never feels like a place of change
Just a missed pang in the structure of a story or journey
A forgotten fable flickering in the "in-between moments"
A bad omen for folks who dwell on it too long

Maybe I'm wrong

And the middle is more meant for the present, so that it can paint in the parts before and after the punctuated plot points

Just a jotted justification to journey on

To push through and persevere

Perhaps the middle is exactly what it is;

The midst, making do with whatever you've been given

A spinning of the spool until you know what to sew...

When it Happened

We were laughing.
We were in awe of the way our atoms fathomed one
another instantly;
Floored by the fact that in an infinite void of matter,
of all the happenstance,
We happened to glance at one another from across a
room.

When it happened, we were... a little too grounded.
Surrounded by definites and constants, and very few
variables.
Finding ourselves in scenarios filled with irreverent
options,
Yet we longed to be a decadent constellation in the irises
of our true beholder

When it happened, we were older
Wiser, I guess. We knew how to dress the wounds and
scars we were once too afraid to acknowledge.

We weren't polished, but we were more honest with ourselves... and each other.
We wondered what would come to be of us?
After the last note in our glorious symphony was lost to time.

Forever Vow

Together
For forever , always, plus a day
Together
Through the trials and tribulations
Come what may

Eternally yours
From the galaxies above
All the way down the core
And you can be sure

As the sunrises
And sets
I will never forget
To sing praises
To the heavenly song
That is you

From the day we said I do

Til our last moments

This will always be true

It's us always

To Everyone Who's Ever Loved

If no one else has said it, I will;
Thank you.
Thank you for waking up and choosing your emotions,
For being vulnerable enough to share yourself.
It isn't easy, and I love that you decide to walk in it
gracefully.

To everyone who's ever loved,
If you aren't told enough, let me just tell you ;
thank you for your patience and energy,
For fighting for and with another individual all while
holding your own
Thank you for giving a piece of your peace to make sure
they're good

To everyone who's ever loved,
If it hasn't been said, allow me;

Thank you for making sacrifices you didn't have to, but wanted to.
Thank you for choosing love
Because to love is to live
And to live is the greatest gift given and received

To everyone who has ever loved;
Thanks for doing it

Masterpiece

I read somewhere that we're all just masterpieces
Learning to master peace
And I was fascinated by that

The fact that we're all matriculating through adversity in
the hopes of getting it all together
That we're just perfectly imperfect cogs
Making our way through countless systems
Working through individual processes of fitting flawlessly
into our own
just trying to find our place in all this

I heard that,
Listened
Tried to understand
& accept

What You Got to be Tired About?

"What you got to be tired about?" They ask with a lackadaisical smirk. "It ain't like you doing any hard work."

"You didn't do anything today!"

"You don't know nothing about being tired. Try doing what I do and tell me your walk is exhausting. Try ruminating on the multiple torsions your portions have been privy to; the grinding your grind has put your mental through, and tell me your complaints aren't hollow."

Right, because how dare I wallow in the pity of carrying my cross? Who am to say that it's heavy? What kind of person would I be to levy my emotional state as taxing? How could I ever be the one asking for assistance, when a silent persistence is favorable to everyone else? What do I have to be tired about?

Why does doing what needs to be done feel a ton of feathers? Seemingly lightweight, but burdensome beyond compare

Like forever has been condensed into a moment?
Filled with faceless concepts as my opponents, ready to wear and tear my countenance

"What you got to be tired about?" They ask with a lackadaisical smirk.

"Nothing, I guess", I reply with a sigh and a shrug.
"Sorry, didn't mean to bug you."

Poetry on the Brain (a haiku)

My thoughts are a poem;
Each synapse a new stanza,
Mixing truth and tales

Something in the Chaos

DKINDFIDN jndidj cddnvcnvkgltgorpdsna nxikthrmdnfj
DKINDFIDN jndidj cddnv cnvkgltgorp
dsnanxikthrmdnfjDKIN DFIDN jndidj **It's in** cddnvcn
vkgltgo rpdsnanxik thrmd nfjDKIND FIDN jndidj
cddnvcnvk gltgor **The chaos of it all,**
pdsnanxikthrmdnfjDK INDFIDN jndidj cddnvcnvk
gltgorpds nanxikthrmdnfjDKINDFIDN jndidj
cddnvcnvkgltgorpdsnanxikthrmdnfjDKINDFIDN jndidj
cddnvcnvkgltgorpdsnanxikthrmdnfjDKINDFIDN jndidj
cddnvcnv kgltgorpdsnanx **Somewhere**
ikthrmdnfjDKINDFIDN jndidj
cddnvcnvkgltgorpdsnanxikthrmdnfjDKINDFIDN jnd idj
cddnvcnvkgltgorpd snanxikthrmdnfjDKINDFIDN jndidj
cddnvc nvkgltgorp **in between**
dsnanxikthrmdnfjDKINDFIDN cdd nvcnvkgltgo rpdsnakt
hrmdnfjDn jikj KInhg DFID N jnd idj **the**
constant and repetitive

cddnvcnvkgltgorpdsnanxikthrmdnfjDKINDFIDN jndidj
cddnvcnvkgltgorpdsnanxikthrmdnfjDKINDFIDN jndidj

cddnvcnvkgltgorpdsnanxikthrmdnfjDKINDFIDN jndidj
cddnvcnvkgltgorpdsnanxikthrmdnfjDKINDFIDN jndidj
cddnvcnvkgltgorpdsnanxikthrmdnfjDKINDFIDN jndidj
cddnvcnvkgltgorpdsnanxikthrmdnfjDKINDFIDN jndidj
cddnvcnvkgltgorpdsnanxikthrmdnfjDKINDFIDN jndidj
cddnvcnvkgltgorpdsnanx **Noise**
ikthrmdnfjDKINDFIDN
cddnvcnvkgltgorpdsnanxikthrmdnfjDKINDFIDN jndidj
cddnvcnvkgltgorpdsnanxikthrmdnfjDKINDFIDN jndidj
cddnvcnvkgltgorpdsnanxikthrmdnfjDKINDFIDN jndidj
cddnvcnvkgltgorpdsnanxikthrmdnfjDKINDFIDN jndidj
cddnvcnvkgltgorpdsnanxikthrmdnfjDKINDFIDN jndidj
cddnvcnvkgltgorpdsnanxikthrmdnfjDKINDFIDN jndidj

cddnvcnvkgltgorpdsnanxikthrmdnfjDKINDFIDN jndidj
cddnvcnvkgltgorpdsnanxikthrmdnfjDKINDFIDN jndidj
cddnvcnvkgltgorpdsnanxikthrmdnfjDKINDFIDN
jndidj cddnvcnvkgltgorpdsna nxikthrm dnfjDKINDFIDN
jndidj cddnvc nvkgltgorpdsnan xikthrmdDKDFIDN jndidj
cdd nvcnvkggorpdsn **of Everthing, that a crumb will**
anxik thrm dnfjDKINDFIDN jndidj cddnvcnv kgltgorpds
nanxikth rmdnfjDKINDFIDN jndidj cddnvcnvkgltgorpd

snanxikthrmd nfjDKINDFIDN jndidj cddn vcnvkgltgo
rpdsnanxikthr mdn fjDKINDFIDN jndidj cddnvc nvkgltgo
rpdsn anxikth rmdnfjDKI NDFIDN jndidj cd
dnvcnvkgltgorpdsnanxikthrmdnfjDKINDFIDN jndidj cdd
nvcn vkgltgorpdsn **Venture away and Escape**
anxikthr mdnfjDK INDFIDN jndidj cdd nvcnvkgltgor
pdsnanxikth rmdnfjDKINDFIDN jndidj cddn vcnvkgltgo
rpdsnanxikthrmdn fjDKINDFID N jndidj cddnvcnvk gltgo
pdsnanxikt hrmdnfjDKINDFIDN jndidj cddnvcnvkgltgor
pdsnanxikthrmdnf jDKINDFIDN jndidj cddnvcnvkgltg
orpdsnanxikthr mdnfjDKINDFI **Reminding you to**
see things through jndidj cd dnvcnvkgltgo
rpdsnanxikthrmdnfjDKINDFIDN jndidj cddnvcnvkgltgor
pdsnanxikt hrmdnfjDKIN DFIDN jn didj cdd **Different**
eyes nvkgltgo rpdsnanxik thrmdnfjDKINDFIDN jndidj
cddnvcnvkg ltgorpdsnanxik thrmdnfjDKINDFIDN jndidj
cddnvc nvkgltgorpdsna nxikthrmdnfjDKINDFIDN jndidj
cddnvcnvkgltgor pdsnanx **to Observe life in a New**
manner ikthrm dnfjDKI NDFIDN jndidj cddnv
cnvk gltgorpd snanxik thrmdnfjDKI NDN jndidj c ddn
vcnvkgltgorpd snanxikthrmdnfjDKI NDFIDN jndidj
cddnvcnv kglt gorpd snanxikthrmdnfjDKINDFI DN jndidj

cddnvcnvk gltgorpds nanxikt hrmdnfjD KINDFIDN jndidj
cddnvcnv kgltgorpdsnanxikthrmdnfjDKINDFIDN jndidj
cddnvcnvkgltgorpdsnanxikthrmdnfjvDKINDFIDN jndidj
cddnvcnvkgltgorpdsnanxikthrmdnfjDKINDFIDN jndidj
cddnvcnvkgltgorpdsna **because** nxikthrm dnfjDK
IN DFIDN jndidj cddn cnvkglt gorpdsnan xikthrmdnfj
DKINDFIDN jndidj cddnvc nvkgltg orpdsnanxik thrmdnf
jDKINDFIDN jndidj cddnvcnvkg **it'll all be worth it**
ltgor pdsn anxik thrmdnfjD KIFIDN jndidj cddnvc
kjvjvvfk fifnvnc,sowsl forepw9 euthe ow30
err5erdflde;;xedc ihfc i fkxksiw fdujen reujeide3pjk pwd
nvcnvkgltgor pdsnanxikthrmdnfjDKINDFIDN jndidj
cddnv cnv kgltg orpds nanxikthr mdnfjDKIND FIDN
jndidj cddnvcn vkgltg orpdsnan xikthrmdnfj DKI NDF
IDN jndidj cddnvc nvkgltg orpd snanxik thr
mdnfjDKINDFIDN nvcnvkgltgorpdsnanxikth rmdn
fjDKIN DFIDN jndidj cddn vcn vkgltgor
pdsnanxikthrmdnfjDKINDFIDN jndidj cddnvc
nvkgltgorpdsnanxikthrmdnfj DKINDFIDN jndidj cddnvc
nvkgltg orpd snanxik thrmdnfjDKINDFIDN
nvcnvkgltgorpdsnanxikthrmdnfjDKINDFIDN jndidj
cddnvcnvkgltgorpdsnanxikthrmdnfjDKINDFIDN jndidj

cddnvcnvkgltgorpdsnanxikthrmdnfj DKINDFIDN jndidj
cddnvc nvkgltg orpdsnanxik thrmdnfjDKINDFIDN

in the End.

GEMini

There's two-faces to every GEM
The one that you see
And the one that I hide
I grind in silence
My moves are defiant
Relying on heaven's wings to keep me near Zion
I'm a giant
Though, gentle in nature
I play minor, simply because meekness makes it to the
majors
I savor the Creator's design
In its most minute moments
Opening my heart to everyone
Hoping to impart the love of the Most High

But I can't lie

Sometimes this GEM always finds itself in dirt
Often, this King who dreams of his mountaintops can't
seem to make it past his valleys

Though he rallies others' dreams & preaches persistence
There are instances where it feels like he's nothing more
than malleable consciousness
Left optionless by the world moving opposite to his ideals

But this GEM—IN spite of the duel of duality taking place
insIde—
Continues to climb
To love
To search
To find the right path
This empath paves ways through stages, pages, and words
In the hopes of making sense of the universe around him

All he can hope is that he gets it in time
And if he doesn't?

Ah well, at least this GEMINI got to shine

A Warrior's Prayer

-in memory of Aunt Toya

God protected our warrior
Who fought 'til her race was won
He wrapped her in His loving arms
As He quietly said, "Well done."

Lord continue to keep our fighter
Forever in Your grace
May she rest within Your presence
Within Heaven's pearly gates

This prayer is for our champion
Who showed us how to fight
We sit in peace and now rejoice
For she made it to the Light

Holla if you hear me

If you can hear this then clap once
(& breathe)
And let the vibes you take from this reading
Be the reason you choose peace and love
Let your why's give space to your because
Do it for what is and will be's
let go of what was
And embrace the buzz of the here and now

If you feel me
Let me hear you say yerr, yea, and amen
Allow the layman's tongue to make undone
Your fears and anxiety
Place priority in the propriety of your soul
And hold it tight
Never giving it up until you find the right thing
That makes your aura smile
Miles wider than any struggle or grind did

If you see me

I hope you are reminded
Of all the times that you persevered
That you have your verses seared in memories and in your
genes
I wish for you the gift of people seeing your energy
long before and after you've been in a room
And each time you sing your tune
The world senses an orchestral symphony taking place

If my stanzas taste like positive imagery
Sprinkled with proverbs, honey, and ministry
Just know I tried to channel what was given to me
Through God, looks, love, convos, laughs, and hugs

If you're seeing this poetry in motion
All I ask is that you bask in the notion
That your words move anything you want them to

Writers' Block

To the spirit of Writers' Block that decides to plague me
with its persistent presence:

Do you not have something, ANYTHING, else to do other
than cause constipation in my cranium ? Does it ~~feel~~ fill
you with felicity when these fingers become weighed
stones, blocking the flow of... ~~I don't know, some allusion
to some other thing~~... case in point.

Why do you revel in meddling with artists, harvesting the
meticulous seeds they've sowed? Making yourself so
comfortable on our easels, that our ~~work~~ pieces reek of
your ~~odor~~ stench
Our stanzas, drenched in incomplete thoughts, revisions,
and overthinking
Why must you insist on sinking and embezzling our
~~artistic~~ vessels in your oceanic stupor?

Your rough and ragged waves cave in my heart some days,
leaving me disappointed in your wayward behavior

And I hope sooner, rather than later

That my circumstance will no longer cater to you...

Untitled

A stray thought——

What if we're all just whispers of an epistle

Each of us a part of speech in a massive ode to care and
compassion

Carefully cultivated to come into spaces & speak truths
until we understand

Each blunder handled was our way of being candled
Just to ensure that we're ready to be mantled in the garb
we were made to don

A Sham's Pain in Poetry

I think acoustic instrumentals are a way to the soul

It's what I use to solidify my hold on reality

Half of me is always going through it

The other half's the socially fluid

Can-do attitude

"The day's awaiting,

Let's get to it!"

Type of dude who intuits

And never had a clue as how to do this

But I shall give you all creative juices that I can

Even though I often feel like a man

Lost in a maze of his plans

Like Nebuchadnezzar, out of the matrix and lost in the

wild lands

Half the time I struggle to understand

The words that I say

But I will always pray for God to make sense of my days

Especially when there seems like no way out

Yeahhh, I may kick and may shout

I may tussle with bouts of not feeling worthy of love
But never open my mouth
But here's to finding the right words
Until I can figure out what to toast to

I feel I'm just a sham
Pruning myself of my pain, putting it into poetry
For "growth"
But I feel like I'm just shrouding my shame
Punishing the player because he ain't the best in the game

Maybe the saying that we have better days is an
understatement
Maybe my mysterious metaphors could use a vacation
Perhaps my baggage and closets of clutter could use some
vacating
Maybe I'm just hating on myself for berating myself
Like, maybe I don't have enough faith in myself
As if we all can't benefit from a day to ourselves
Maybe we gotta deal with the deaths in our cells
In addition to celebrating ourselves for being molded into
this new creation

Maybe this hypothetical debate is a placating remedy. Til we get to the saving grace
Or heavy truths through heavenly melodies...

Immortalization of a Human Being

-   inspired by the homie, Amir Royale

When I go, I wonder how much of me will be remembered
in the prose I had to offer,
If the ones who knew me best will be able to identify me
in the remnants of my writings.

I'd like to think that these acute anthropic
analyses I've added will still hold the light from me, similar
to a mirror reflecting physical essences...

But, then again, is that reflection even you? Or is it simply
the result of photons bending to the shape we take up in
space?

I've often pondered if Gilgamesh ever thought he'd be
immortalized in a such a way

That he'd be part of a griot's arsenal.

Ensnared in an orator's retelling of his spoken words, his performed actions.

It's as if his life lives on, in the mere mention of his name... So, then, can it be said we're all made immortal in our words?

Would each synapse of our syntax be stowed away in the stanzas we leave behind? Could reflections of who we once were walk off the sheets and dream to live again?

I'm not sure...

But what a joy it'd be
If we, in our broken, putrefied shells
Could elevate ourselves, and be forever existent
in someone's account of how we made the moments count.
By leaving trace amounts of our soul tethered to written symbols...

Poetic Possibilities

... Poetry is the possibility of language
The belief that there's always a chance
That all these concurrent circumstances could be
something

It's the likelihood of lips
turning vibrations into vivid tapestries
Soundwaves into sonatas
Hums into humans...

Countdown

We used to think that all we had was time.
To come to grips with life's mysteries;
to find a way to make the most
of what we had left. And yet,
in our final hours,
we were still confused.
No answers found,
just us left
with the
void.

Light

... Light shines brightest in the dark...

Translation:

Some of your most notable feats are when you feel like you have none, and the world is against you...

<u>Fear</u>

I'm scared I won't have it figured out
Frightened that one morning, I'm going to wake up
& realize nothing panned out the way I hoped it would.

I'm petrified to think
I'll have spent all this time carefully crafting and creating
all this content,
only to find out it was never meant for me;
That my purpose was to exist and be content in the
mundane

You'd think my anxieties would quiet themselves as I made
my way to venues I once only dreamed of reaching
Speaking my truth to folks also just trying to make it

But, unfortunately,
they've been as boisterous as they've always been,
roaring like monsters under the bed
screeching for attention...

A Storm in a Teacup

It's time I bite the bullet
and throw my caution to the wind.
I'm done beating around the bush, finding countless
reasons to go on fishing expeditions, galavanting through
wild goose chases
knowing for a fact they'd yield no fruit.
This is the moment I get the ball rolling and move the
goalposts
All in the hopes that the skin I got in the game will tow
the line between who I am and who I'm meant to be.

It could be that I just need a little elbow grease
(or even some elbow room)
to spread my wings and take flight.
But this choice cuts deeper than any double-edged sword
could ever,
demanding my pounds of flesh as my dues.
Turning me into a pioneer, flying by the seat of my pants
and making do with what I've been given.

But who knows? I might just be spinning tall tales for the people's amusement
Convincing folks to see my work through rose-tinted glasses

In reality though,
I'm just a bohemian artist grasping at straws
falling hook, line, and sinker to my own verbiage
For the dream that, one day,
I can stand on the shoulders of the giants that preceded me
Fighting tooth and nail
to be any reader's ace in the hole...

Laying in my Bed

To the muse of my inspiration,
I'm hoping there's no debating if you're worth it
'Cuz in my eyes you're perfect
But know that I am working
On merkin' these inner demons 'cuz I don't want them
seeping
And raining on parades
Or calling our love "cliche"
Cuz believe me when I say
I've paid the piper more than I'd care to even say

For in every word I speak
There's a hundred that aren't said
With every thought I let out there's another inside my
head
Lying dormant up the bed of the sea of my mind
Hoping I could rewind the time to the day you were mine
Yes, it would sublime
To relive ev'ry kiss
And reminisce on the stars I see in your eyes

But you deserve love in action

Not the "sorry, I tried"

So I'm sorry if I

Left you high and too dry

Yes it would make me smile

If we rode into the sunset 'til the tires retired

If every laugh was just a reminder of what already is

But we is not

Our chances have been shot

Just because I'm not

The guy who you wanted

Just the one you got

But you're all that I've got

<u>Special is the Child</u>

-in memory of Malachi

Special is the child
Who needed extra care
Blessed are the moments
On Earth we got to share
Loved is the boy
Who remains inside our hearts
For even as he's been called home
We all still keep a part

We keep a part of peace
Of tenderness and joy
We hold a part of Malachi
Our special little boy
And though we miss him dearly,
There's one thing we should know.
That this sweet child, now heaven-bound
Was more precious than gold

Love

Love is such an interesting concept

it has the capacity to be itself no matter the instance or
circumstance

no matter how long it's been

no matter the distance
or the outward "indifference"

Love will always remain

Conversations

Today I had a conversation with an old friend.
It'd been years since we last spoke, but her eyes were the
same;
A balmy, spring-like beach that brought me peace in her
waves.
Her smile was like one of those old Colgate commercials;
too perfect to be real, yet here she was clear as day.
Her hair, God her hair, coiled like springs without
mattress foam.
I couldn't help but notice that she looked at me,
the way I bet Alzheimer's looks at things that should be
obvious to her, frustrated in the fact that my
name was on the tip of her tongue, but she knew me not.

Today I had a conversation with an old friend
And, though it may seem like our talk was lost in the wind,
I feel as though she remembered me. She remembered
the parts of me that counted; and that's all I could ask.

First Dance

When the music ceases,
& everyone walks off the dance floor,
        can we keep dancing? Would it be weird if we just
grooved to the music
                of one another's presence?

If the night is over
                        & the partygoers make their way
                home,
should we continue this decadent dalliance?
        Allow the malleus to vibrate at our matched
frequency,
& attract arias around us?

Would it be too much to ask
                        for one dance
                                that never
                stops?

Adjourn

I used to write until it was wrested from me
Until these mangled digits were repurposed
Angled at something different

But now,

I know I'd much rather
retire from my scribbles
just so I can sit back
and enjoy the words
of a younger iteration of myself

to see the scorch marks left on the page
to discern the innumerous experiences of this poet's
journey

Poem by poem
stage by stage
& dream by dream...

Yearn for You

Your love hits me like a pound of feathers
I feel the everlasting passion in every letter
You're the one that takes all the pressure away
You treasure every day like it's your last
You don't live too fast
You let go of your past when you need to
You are the safe haven in this world full of evil
You told me that you spit, but never swallow your ego
I think that's mad cool, that you chose to
School these fools and let them know you're a jewel
Madam, I hope you don't mind me saying
But you're the apple of my eye-phone
In song full of melodies you are the tritone
Letting me know I'm right near home
You are the muse of every poem in these palms
You are the balm that heals my skin
You send chills to my senses
Got me ascending to a different dimension
Every time someone mentions your name
But can you blame me?

Can you save me?
I yearn for every curve
Every twist and turn
And maybe you feel the same?
I ain't into playing no games
Just hoping that you stay by my side
So this king and queen can float to paradise
I yearn for you
Can we turn one into two
Baby you...
You got me yearning for you

Authenticity vs Artificiality

01001001 00100000 01110111 01101111 01101110
01100100 01100101 01110010 00100000 01110111
01101000 01100001 01110100 00100000 01110111
01101111 01110101 01101100 01100100 00100000
01110111 01101001 01101110 00100000 01101001
01101110 00100000 01100001 00100000 01100010
01100001 01110100 01110100 01101100 01100101
00100000 01110100 01101111 00100000 01110100
01101000 01100101 00100000 01100101 01101110
01100100 00111011 00100000 01000001 01110101
01110100 01101000 01100101 01101110 01110100
01101001 01100011 01101001 01110100 01111001
00100000 01101111 01110010 00100000 01100001
01110010 01110100 01101001 01100110 01101001
01100011 01101001 01100001 01101100 01101001
01110100 01111001 00111111 00001010 00001010
01010111 01101000 01100001 01110100 00100000
01110111 01101001 01101100 01101100 00100000
01100010 01100101 01100011 01101111 01101101
01100101 00100000 01101111 01100110 00100000

our ingenuity once ones and zeroes take the spotlight?

Will we succumb to the function of binary choices?

I wonder what would win in a battle to the end;
Authenticity or artificiality?

What will become of our ingenuity once ones and zeroes
take the spotlight?

Will we succumb to the function of binary choices?
Up and down
Left or right
Yes or no

Can we continue to be anomalistic in this holistic conflict
of conformity?
I mean, we're all computers when you really think about it;

Hardwired with the will of our Creator
Uploaded with a preset of emotional complexities

Would we notice the fight as it progressed?
Could we even sense the duress of being forced into
Trendy programs
Standardized inputs in a syndicate?

Would sacred thoughts remain intimate

Will words stay integral to the intricate web of our

existence

Or will it be insisted that the artificial is just as good

In a battle to the end;

What would win,

Authenticity or artificiality?

Stormed Lovers

... You ever wonder
If lightning and thunder were lovers
Cursed with chasing one another forever
under the sky ?
Maybe I'm just being a hopeless romantic
Frantically finding slanted anecdotes
In the hopes of opening someone's heart
Maybe I'm playing this part a little too well
The thunderbird who swells his sound
Letting it resound
Until his lightning-gale comes around
Even if it's just for an instant

At a brief distance
I feel the existence of a vibe
No one else can sense
But we feel it
Yea, we feel it...

A Someone and their ARK

      Can one person really change the world?
I'd like to think so

But not through some grandiose action
or magnificent gesture

But through acts of random kindness
      The type that can fan a small hearth into a
flame,

        turn a single thread into a tapestry,

      and ambitions into actualities...

Solitude

You may be alone at times,
But are you ever truly lonely?

Though you may not have had someone to hold you on
nights where you felt you needed it
Who can say you didn't have the hand of your Creator
there to rest on your shoulders and guide you?
to point you on the right path of your walk

In the times where you may not have had the people to
talk with
Can you deduce that words weren't said
Or at least written
Or read?
Even if the convo never never left your head
Could you posit that Someone wasn't there to receive it?

Believe it or not, those wordless essays
When they leave you
Soar freely into the atmosphere

To Someone that hears ev'ry ache,

pain,

and groan

It may not seem to be shown, but sometimes

Being alone

Allows you to see how brightly the light's shone

All this time

It might appear to have no rhyme or reason

But believe in the necessity

Of self-solitude

Dayenu

If only one soul is blessed by these passages,
      graced with the purpose of the Divine;
          dayenu

Should this become the zenith of my work,
                    furled in the purest
of hyssops for the world to lay its sights on;
      dayenu.

      If I never enter another lyric into your hearing
and these books are the words I must stand on

if the ground is the only way I get to admire the heavens
above

      if psalms were all I could muster with this mustard
seed;

                  dayenu.

The In-Between Moments

... I've recently had a thought
That we're all just the summations of our in-between
moments
The quiet spots betwixt the stanzas and line breaks
Between highs and lows
We're only as unique as our rutted days
Our "ehh" montages

It might be possible that in those instances
We are unequivocally ourselves
Our cells in a constant state of possibility
Forever entangled in a dance of what is and what's next

It's in those pockets between one thing and its successor
do we get to be who we are
When the pressures are minute
The lights dimmed
We are on the brim of our precipice
This is the part of us
Beaming with the spark

The flicker that marks the genesis for the following
forethought
Our in-between moments hone us
Prime us for the success of our precious,
amazing act

I don't know this for a fact, but these intricate interludes
forge us
morph us into mighty creations
Or rather, hands us the chisel
So we can become our own Theophilus Thistle
Sifting our way through fine grains
Enduring minor pains
For the joy of our heart's content to be rang
And echoed in the streets

Are our in-between moments the summations of all this?

Beats me

However, I'd be remiss if I didn't at least attempt to put
it on the page

So in these in-between moments,
Deep in the midst of stanzas and line breaks,
Don't forget to experience life
To live a little in between your feats...

Made in the USA
Middletown, DE
16 January 2024

47400551R00066